Big Mouse, Little Mouse

Written by Jill Eggleton
Illustrated by Stella Yang

Rigby

The mice in the book

Big Mouse

Little Mouse

The kitchen in the book

Big Mouse said to
Little Mouse,

"I'm going to get
some food.
You stay here.
A **big** cat is
in the kitchen."

Big Mouse went out of
the hole and into the kitchen.
His nose went...

SNIFF,

SNIFF,

SNIFF!

He looked in the cabinet.

"**Yum, food!**" said Big Mouse.

Big Mouse will get...

apple Yes? No?

cheese Yes? No?

cake Yes? No?

Big Mouse had cheese
and bread and cake.
Then he went back to the hole.

"Where's my food?"
said Little Mouse.

"No food," said Big Mouse.
"There's no food
in the house!"

Big Mouse went to sleep.
When he woke up,
he said to Little Mouse,

"I'm going to
look for food.
You stay here.
Two big cats are
in the kitchen."

Big Mouse went out of
the hole and into the kitchen.
His nose went...

SNIFF,

SNIFF,

SNIFF!

He looked on the table.

"**Yum, food!**" said Big Mouse.

Big Mouse will get...

bread  Yes? No?

carrot Yes? No?

chips Yes? No?

Big Mouse had bread
and chips.
Then he went back to the hole.

"Where's my food?"
said Little Mouse.

"No food," said Big Mouse.
"There's no food
in the house."

Big Mouse went to sleep.
When he woke up, he said,

"I'm going to look for food."

But Big Mouse had gotten very fat!

16

"**Help**," he said.
"I can't get out of this hole."

"I will go then," said Little Mouse.
"I'm not scared of cats!"

Little Mouse went into the kitchen.

"There are no cats here," he said.
"I will have a party."

Little Mouse will have...

tomato Yes? No?

popcorn Yes? No?

Little Mouse took some popcorn back to Big Mouse.

Big Mouse said, "Thank you, Little Mouse. You are very kind!"

"There **is** food in the house," said Little Mouse.
"**I** will get it from now on. I'm not scared of cats!"

The End

Party Food for Mice

popcorn

chips

cake

bread

cheese

Party Food for Me

cake Yes? No?

apple Yes? No?

chips  Yes? No?

tomato Yes? No?

carrot  Yes? No?

Word Bank

bread

cabinet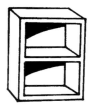

cake

cheese

chips

hole

kitchen

nose

popcorn

table